BOBO

DOMES OF
FABEDOUGOU

MOU FOREST

A note from the author

The southwest of Burkina Faso is one of my favorite places in the world. You can splash in cool water at the Karfiguéla falls, watch hippos at Tengréla Lake, or climb the gigantic egg-shaped rock domes of Fabedougou. Those domes are 1.8 billion years old. That's right, ONE POINT EIGHT BILLION.

Riding in chock-full minibuses is not the most comfortable way to see Africa, but it's definitely the most fun. And it's even more fun if you get to ride ON TOP of the bus like Fatima and Galo, with the wind in your hair and plenty of animals to look after.

I wrote *All Aboard for the Bobo Road* for my friends in Banfoura and Bobo Dioulasso. I hope that they (and you) enjoy this colorful journey on the most beautiful road in the world!

For Daisy – S.D.
To Hendrik and Rune – C.C.

American edition published in 2016 by Andersen Press USA, an imprint of Andersen Press Ltd. • www.andersenpressusa.com • First published in Great Britain in 2016 by Andersen Press Ltd., 20 Vauxhall Bridge Road, London SW1V 2SA.

Text copyright © Stephen Davies, 2016. Illustration copyright © Christopher Corr, 2016. All rights reserved. No part of this book may be reproduced, stored in a retrieval system, or transmitted in any form or by any means—electronic, mechanical, photocopying, recording, or otherwise—without the prior written permission of Andersen Press Ltd., except for the inclusion of brief quotations in an acknowledged review.

Distributed in the United States and Canada by Lerner Publishing Group, Inc. 241 First Avenue North, Minneapolis, MN 55401 USA • For reading levels and more information, look up this title at www.lernerbooks.com.

Color separated in Switzerland by Photolitho AG, Zürich. Printed and bound in China. Library of Congress Cataloging-in-Publication Data Available.

ISBN: 978-1-5124-1598-8   eBook ISBN: 978-1-5124-1599-5   1-TL-6/1/16

ALL ABOARD FOR THE BOBO ROAD

Stephen Davies   Christopher Corr

ANDERSEN PRESS USA

At the Banfora bus station a crowd of chattering passengers are climbing aboard Big Ali's minibus.

"All aboard for the Bobo Road!" Big Ali booms.

"The most beautiful road in the world!"

High up on the roof of the minibus, helping to load the luggage, are Big Ali's children Fatima and Galo. Going to Bobo is a special treat and they are both very excited.

BEEP, BEEP — they're off!

The wheels
of the minibus
go round.

"Enjoy the ride!" Big Ali booms. "Next stop, Lake Tengréla."
Fatima and Galo are riding on the roof. They like looking after
the luggage and feeling the wind on their faces.

Beside the hippo lake, the bus
slows down and stops.

There are people to board and luggage to load:
two mopeds and three bicycles. Fatima and
Galo use ropes to tie them down.

BEEP, BEEP! They're off again.

"Goodbye, hippos!"
Big Ali booms. "Next stop,
Karfiguéla Falls."

Beside the waterfall, the bus slows down and stops.
There are more people to board and luggage to load:
four cans of cooking oil and five sacks of rice.

BEEP,
BEEP!
They're off again.

"Hold on tight," Big Ali booms. "Next stop, the Domes of Fabedougou."

In the shadow of the old rock domes,
the bus slows down and stops. There are
even more people to board and luggage to load:
six enormous yams and seven watermelons.
"Don't eat those melons, Galo!" says Fatima.
"They're not for you."

And then — BEEP, BEEP!
They're off again.

"I told you this road is beautiful,"
booms Big Ali. "Next stop, the magical
Forest of Mou."

In the middle of the deep, dark forest, the bus slows down and stops. This time the luggage is alive!

Eight ducks, nine goats, and ten chickens. Fatima and Galo make the animals comfortable. And then — BEEP, BEEP! They're off again. "Next stop, Bobo!" booms Big Ali.

The minibus heads out of the forest and into a big city. "Hooray!" shouts Fatima. "We're here!"

They judder by fruit stalls and a caterpillar café,

past the train station, and the Grand Mosque.

Finally, they arrive at Bobo station.

"Everybody off!"

Wheezing and sneezing, Fatima and Galo
help Big Ali to unload ten chickens,
nine goats, and eight ducks.
A donkey cart is waiting to take
the animals to market.

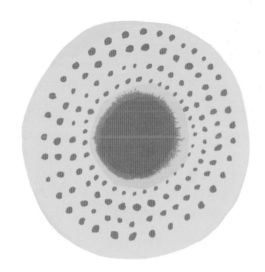

Huffing and puffing, Galo unloads
seven watermelons and six enormous yams.
Some women take the fruit and vegetables.
"Now we can set up our stall," they say.

Craning and straining, Fatima unloads five sacks of rice and four cans of cooking oil.

"Thank you," says a man. "Now I can open my restaurant."

Tired and hungry,
the children help
Big Ali to unload
three bicycles and
two mopeds.

"Thank you," say their owners.
"See you again soon."

All the luggage has been taken away, except for just one thing:
the big, round, mysterious package wrapped in cloth and string.
"Look!" says Fatima. "I wonder who that belongs to?"
"It belongs to you two," booms Big Ali. "You deserve it."
They open up the big, round package...

...and inside is a huge pot
of rice, beans, and fried fish!

Fatima and Galo wash their hands
and sit down around the pot
with their father.

"Another beautiful sight,"
breathes Big Ali,
gazing at the sunset.
"Yes," say the children,
gazing at the pot,
"and it's delicious too!"

LAKE
TENGRÉLA

KARFIGUÉLA
FALLS

GURUNSI
HOUSES

BANFORA

31901060081801